SIDEKICKS

SIDEKICKS

by Dan Danko and Tom Mason

Illustrated by Barry Gott

LITTLE, BROWN AND COMPANY

New York ↝ An AOL Time Warner Company

First Edition

The characters and events portrayed in this book are fictitious. Any
similarity to real persons, living or dead, is coincidental and not
intended by the author.

CIP data is available.
ISBN (pb) 0-316-16844-0
ISBN (hc) 0-316-16845-9

10   9   8   7   6   5   4   3   2   1
LAKE

Printed in the United States of America

The text for this book was set in Bookman Old Style, and
the display type is Bernhard Gothic.

To Jack Kirby, the king who showed us
how to dream with our eyes open

SIDEKICKS

LEAGUE OF BIG JUSTICE
BATTLE JOURNAL — DAY 1

Pumpkin Pete spilled pâté on his super tux at the mayor's inauguration. Spent day scrubbing spot from shirt and doing laundry. Did homework. Watched TV.

LEAGUE OF BIG JUSTICE
BATTLE JOURNAL — DAY 2

Washed Pumpkinmobile. Did homework. Watched TV.

LEAGUE OF BIG JUSTICE
BATTLE JOURNAL — DAY 3

Listened to Charisma Kid's stupid story about how he and King Justice saved the world. (Again.) Ironed Pumpkin Pete's super shirt for his date with Lipstick Lydia. Did homework. Watched TV.

LEAGUE OF BIG JUSTICE
BATTLE JOURNAL — DAY 4

Spent whole day trying to get lipstick stains out of Pumpkinmobile upholstery. Did homework. Watched TV.

LEAGUE OF BIG JUSTICE
BATTLE JOURNAL — DAY 5

See Day Two.

LEAGUE OF BIG JUSTICE
BATTLE JOURNAL — DAY 6

Battled the InterNut on top of the Empire State Building. Saved Pumpkin Pete. (Again.) Shot InterNut's fusion web bomb into space. Saved New York. Did homework. Watched TV.

LEAGUE OF BIG JUSTICE
BATTLE JOURNAL — DAY 7

Grounded by Mom and Dad for being out past curfew last night while saving New York. Did homework. No TV.

Chapter One
Evil Never Sleeps In

"What are you tugging at?" Spelling Beatrice asked.

"Nothing!" I said, and stopped tugging.

I hate Spandex. I mean, I guess like a million years ago in the forties when all this superhero stuff really started, it was a cool idea. But man, that crud is always creeping up on you, y'know. Not that you really wanted to know that, but I just had to tell you in case, y'know, you ever see me tugging or something.

"Have you gotten any assignments today?" Spelling Beatrice asked, sitting next to me at the Sidekick Clubhouse Super Computer. Spelling

Beatrice has the typical sidekick outfit. Bright yellow colors that scream "Kidnap me!" That same cruddy Spandex and double-thick glasses that make her look closer to Owl Girl (who looks nothing like an owl and only picked that name because she likes owls). Beatrice is seventeen. She's been a sidekick for almost three years, but what she really wants to do is act.

My sidekick costume is pretty cool. I wear these totally hip goggles to keep the bugs out of my eyes when I run. My outfit is midnight blue with yellow highlights and this glittery lightning bolt striking across my chest.

There isn't much science to being a super-hero sidekick. You have to have a legal waiver from your parent or guardian unless you're eighteen. Ever since that ugly court battle with UnderAge Albert and the child labor laws, it's just plain impossible to become a sidekick without a bundle of legal paperwork.

I'm thirteen now. So once a year, me and my parents have to go file more paperwork. You wanna talk about a life-or-death battle? Try standing in line at City Hall.

The only other thing you needed to be a sidekick is a super power. I run fast. Real fast. Before me, the fastest man alive was Fastest Man

Alive Man. He could run 63.4 miles per hour. I don't know what that is in kilometers. I'm American. We hate metrics.

Except with soda bottles. Those *only* come in metrics. One liter. Hey, don't ask me. I just run fast.

Anyway, Fastest Man Alive Man was the . . . well . . . fastest man alive until I got my powers last year. Now I can run 92.7 miles per hour. Then Fastest Man Alive Man changed his name to Almost Fastest Man Alive Man, but who really cares about the *almost* fastest man alive? I think he retired with about a million leftover boxes of t-shirts that said I LOVE FASTEST MAN ALIVE MAN!

"No assignments worth mentioning, unless you count finding new batteries for Pumpkin Pete's utility gourd," I complained, holding out eight triple-A's.

"I thought that thing was nuclear-powered," Spelling Beatrice commented.

"It was, until he dropped it at the Corn State Mall grand opening in Des Moines and had a core leak." I turned the yellow gourd over and showed her a small crack covered by a Band-Aid.

"Wow. What happened?"

"Let's just say they're calling Iowa 'the Popcorn State' now," I said.

The two of us sat and watched the Sidekick Clubhouse Super Computer monitor. Okay, maybe it wasn't *really* very super and was barely even a computer. It's a Vic-20. If you're wondering what the heck that is, just go to your local computer museum. It'll be the computer they're using as a doorstop.

"No action tonight." I sighed.

"Wanna play Scrabble?" Beatrice asked, pulling the game from her utility backpack. I could already hear those little letter tiles mocking me from inside the box.

"Might as well," I said, nodding. "It beats monitor duty."

And it did. It had only been three weeks since I became a superhero sidekick, but I already knew anything beat monitor duty. You just sit there staring at the monitor waiting for something to happen. They won't call us on our cell phones or pagers. Every day one of us sidekicks has to sit in front of the Vic — I mean Sidekick Super Computer — and wait for a signal from the League of Big Justice. Then, and this is the best part, whoever is on monitor duty when the signal comes in calls all the other sidekicks on their cell phones and tells them to report.

Beatrice unfolded the game and we picked our seven letters.

"Z-I-G-G-U-R-A-T," Beatrice spelled out as she placed down all of her letters in her first turn. "That's nineteen points for the word, fifty for using all my letters at once, and double for going first . . . one hundred and thirty-eight points."

"Wait! How can you spell an eight-letter word when you only have seven letters?" I asked, pointing to the seven tiles she had slapped down on the Scrabble board.

"I *am* Spelling Beatrice."

I should have picked Monopoly.

I looked at my own letters: O-O-O-D-P-A-R. I shuffled them around. O-P-O-R-D-O-A. I shuffled them a third time.

"Do you want some help?" Beatrice inquired.

"No!" I reached down to my tile rack and pulled off a pretty good word. I mean, it's no Zig-guwhatever, but then I'm not a human dictionary, either. "Door. That's four poin —"

"Zwieback. Eighty-six points," Beatrice said, enthusiastically plopping down all seven of her letters again. "That's two hundred thirty-four to four. Hey! You're doing better than last time."

Where's an alien invasion when you really need one? I gotta admit, getting creamed in Scrabble by a girl whose biggest claim to fame was that she actually knows what a dangling participle is, is not really my idea of being a superhero. Or even a superhero sidekick.

I mean, you read all the unofficial biographies and watch all the unofficial movies-of-the-week and it looks all glamorous and stuff. But the truth is, it's more about doing laundry and getting my butt kicked by a girl who thinks proper grammar will save the earth.

Then it happened. It was amazing.

No, not a supervillain attack or some enormous monster rising from the ocean depths to destroy the city. There was no ticking bomb or urgent cry for help from the League of Big Justice. No. What happened was, I picked up the Scrabble board and threw it across the clubhouse.

Then we got the urgent call for help from the League of Big Justice.

"Speedy! Spelling Beatrice! Thank th' bagpipes o' Angus MacGarrnacuuraan! Ah've found ye! Make haste, me twosome! Whar attacked by th' villainous duo Grease an' Grime!"

It was Captain Haggis! His pixilated image flashed briefly on the black and white screen of the Sidekick Super Computer. He sounded urgent, desperate, and then the transmission was cut.

Finally! Some action! And we were his only hope!

"Let's go, Beatrice!" I said, and raced out the door.

I gotta admit, when I get an assignment, it's like my birthday, Christmas, and any other day people give me free stuff wrapped into one. I can't even tell you how cool it is fighting evil. Fighting bad is cool, too. But not as cool as fighting evil, I'll tell you that.

Okay, so most of the time my assignments seemed to involve cleaning things. I don't know what it is about superheroes, but they are the dirtiest people on the planet — and I'm not just talking about The Stain. At least that guy's got an excuse. But I guess that's just what happens when you're the newest sidekick. Not like Charisma Kid. If I could be any sidekick, I would be him.

He's been a sidekick longer than anyone but Sidekick Lad and is kinda the unofficial leader of the Sidekicks; not just because he's the coolest sidekick in, like, the galaxy, but because he's been assigned to the coolest superhero in the universe: King Justice, founder and captain of the League of Big Justice.

"Taking a bite out of crime, one pizza slice at a time." At least that's what King Justice's public relations kit said.

I've only met Charisma Kid once. Well, I didn't actually *meet* him. He kinda walked by me at the sidekicks roll call. He waved to me. Or I think he did. He could've been swatting that fly buzzing around his head, but I'm sure it was like a swatting-wave, you know? Two birds, one stone, and stuff. I'm kinda embarrassed to admit it, but before I became a sidekick, well, I kinda had Charisma Kid's poster on my wall.

Okay, I wasn't one of those geeks who lived in their parents' basement. And I only had three posters. One of Charisma Kid and one of King Justice. The third was of Lipstick Lydia. It was on the inside of my closet door. You know how parents are about that kinda stuff.

It wasn't a far run from the Clubhouse to the League of Big Justice. In fact, the Sidekick Clubhouse was in the deserted lot directly behind the

League of Big Justice and under the city's power cables. Something about property being beneath a jillion volts makes rent cheap and stuff. And everyone figures we're already mutated, so what the heck.

Beatrice and I raced under the League of Big Justice Super Justice Arch and through the League of Big Justice Super Justice Revolving Door. The League of Big Justice Super Justice Lobby was empty.

Okay, I just gotta stop the excitement roller coaster right here for a sec. I mean, this is the League of Big Justice: the most awesome assemblage of superheroes the world has ever known, all under one super roof.

King Justice. Lady Bug. Captain Haggis. The Stain. Mr. Ironic. The Good Egg. Ms. Mime. Depression Dave. The Librarian. And my own sponsor, Pumpkin Pete.

Every time I walk down the Hall of Heroes of Big Justice or past the League of Big Justice Souvenir Gift Shop, a chill runs down my spine. How could it not? Time and time again, these guys bail out the earth from alien invasions, mad scientists, robot armies, evil plots, and just plain nasty people. And now I'm one of them: or at least a sidekick to one of them.

Okay, it's Pumpkin Pete, but hey, we take what we can, right?

What surprise attack would make the League of Big Justice turn to me and Beatrice for help? What could possibly defeat them?

Nothing. That's why my palms were getting so sweaty.

We slapped our hands on the FingerPrintronic. After our prints gave a positive ID, a laser shot out from the wall and scanned our retinas for a positive match.

I could hear the door to the League of Big Justice Inner Sanctum of Justice slide open. I turned and ran directly into the wall. It happens every time. That laser eye scan is like ten grandmas taking pictures with flashbulbs five inches from your face. The big, glowing red spots usually last for two minutes.

Beatrice and I, still half-blind, shuffled into the Inner Sanctum of Justice.

"Hey! Great to see you! You're looking swell." It was Charisma Kid. Even if I was completely blind, I could tell his voice: the voice of honor, the voice of courage, the voice that went with the confidence of a really great smile. "We need your help, Speedy."

Oh . . . my . . . gosh! Did he just say my code name? Charisma Kid — the Charisma Kid — knows who I am!

"Yessir! Speedy! That's —"

"No time for chitchat, rookie!" Charisma cut in. "Are you ready to fight the forces of evil?"

The forces of evil? Oh man! If I thought fighting evil was cool, fighting the forces of *anything* was, like, the ultimate!

"Yessir!" Beatrice and I both enthused back.

The red spots in my eyes began to fade and I could vaguely see CK's (that's what his friends called him) face. I think it's okay for me to call him CK. I *am* one of the inner circle.

"Here," he said, slapping something spongy in my hand. "You'll need this!"

"Shouldn't we wait a few seconds until Beatrice and I can see better?" I asked, worried about battling the forces of evil with a big red spot in the middle of its face.

"Wait? Wait!?" CK exploded with near disgust. "Evil never sleeps in."

Wow. He *was* the coolest.

"I'm a little worried," Beatrice whispered to me as we ran after CK. "I left my Scrabble tiles back at the Clubhouse."

"Befuddle them with some palindromes," I replied.

We burst through some double doors, the three of us, like a trio of horsemen sweeping onto the battlefield carrying the bright waving standards of hope — hope we carried in our hearts and in our hands like a . . . sponge?

I looked into my own hand and that's what I saw. A sponge, slightly soapy.

"Go get 'em!" Captain Haggis called out from a long dinner table, piled with half-eaten food and dessert bowls.

Beatrice and I followed Captain Haggis's pointing finger through a second set of double doors, and there I saw it: the Mount Everest of dishes. The Grand Canyon of grime. The Any-Other-Really-Really-Big-Thing of crusty plates.

"Don't turn your back on that grease!" Charisma Kid chuckled as he left the kitchen and went back to the dining room. "It's a real killer."

Beatrice sighed, picked up a scouring pad, and started scrubbing. "I'll wash. You dry."

I threw the sponge onto the ground and fumed. Today I realized two things. One: Sometimes being a sidekick really stinks. Two: Charisma Kid is a jerk.

Chapter Two
Evil Never Sleeps In — Part II

"I don't know, Guy," Miles said, his cheek full of baloney. "CK is the coolest."

"First of all, the snob only lets his friends call him CK," I corrected. "And secondly, he's a jerk. I'm telling you. After I finished the dishes, he totally started calling me Spuddy even though he knew my name was Speedy."

"Maybe it was a secret code and you missed the cue."

"Yeah. A secret jerk code."

Miles and I have been best friends since the second grade, when I made milk shoot out his nose. We always hang out together at school and when I'm not sidekicking. He's a little chubby, which he says is just baby fat, and has brown hair. He's the only one besides my parents who knows my secret identity.

Not that I want to keep it a secret. Man, if it were up to me, I'd be standing on the top of the school auditorium screaming, "Look at me! Look at me! I'm a superhero sidekick!" until my throat was sore.

Too bad I have parents, huh?

"We don't want some supervillain blowing up our house because you foiled his plan to rule the world, young man," my dad had chastised me when I first became a sidekick.

"What will the neighbors say?" my mom had lamented. "It's bad enough your brother's a florist."

I guess I should be happy that they even let me be a sidekick at all. But what else can you do when you wake up one day and your son can run 92.7 miles per hour?

Miles swallowed the last bite of his sandwich and the lunch bell rang. We threw away our trash and headed off to algebra class. It's not like I wanted to take algebra. Heck, I'd rather be in home ec. At least then I would've gotten free food.

It was my sidekick sponsor's idea.

"You never know," Pumpkin Pete had enthused when I picked my freshman classes. "One day algebra may just save my life."

"What about *my* life?" I had questioned.

"Oh yeah. Yours too, Spuddy."

"Speedy."

"Whatever."

The first thing you did once you became a sidekick was to get a sponsor. All the new sidekicks who had met the rigorous admission standards of the Sidekick Clubhouse — and by "rigorous standards" I mean the check cleared — lined up in a row facing the handful of superheroes who, for reasons that most of us didn't want to know and the insurance company wouldn't let them tell, didn't have a sidekick.

Then, and this is where the real scientific part came in, they picked us like they were picking players for their basketball team.

"Uh . . . that tall guy."

"I pick . . . the one in glasses."

"Let's see? Do you complain? Whine? No? I'll take you."

"Would you be willing to sacrifice your life to save mine?" Pumpkin Pete had asked me as he walked down the line.

"Uh . . . I guess," I replied, not really sure.

"I get this one!" Pete shouted.

Pete is about six-foot-five, with long arms and a thin, lanky body. And, in case you couldn't guess by the name, his head is a pumpkin.

"*I've* got all the powers of a pumpkin," he proudly bragged to me just moments after he picked me.

I'm still trying to figure out what that means.

I sit in algebra class next to Prudence Cane. Don'tcha just love that name? I do. *And* her eyes, her smile, her hair, her smell, and even the way she pretends not to know I exist.

If super beauty were a power, Prudence would be the *Titanic* of gorgeousness. Wait. The *Titanic* sank, didn't it? Okay, she's the *Titanic* before it sank. But thinner. And without the smokestacks.

"Hey, Prudence," I said as I leaned over her desk.

She blew a bubble with her gum and stared at me over the pink edge. "Hey, Gary."

"Guy."

"Whatever." She turned her back to me.

Stupid! Stupid! Stupid! I should've just said my name was Gary! I mean it's just a name, not like I was attached to that "Guy" name anyway.

"Guy? Guy?" Miles asked. "What are you doing?"

"Shut up. My name's Gary."

This is what really kills me about keeping my powers secret. If I just told her the truth, just once, that I could win every track event, be the best basketball player in the school, score a touchdown every time I touch a football, she'd love me. She'd think I was as awesome as I thought she was.

Instead, I was sitting in algebra class wishing my name was Gary.

Maybe if I used my powers a little and stuff. Y'know, nothing really big, but just enough to be more popular. Would that be such a bad thing? I once read that with great power comes great responsibility. My power's not *that* great, so do I really have to be *that* responsible?

The good thing was, now that I'd totally embarrassed myself in front of Prudence, I didn't think my life could get any worse.

"Class," Mr. Lang, the algebra teacher, said, "I'd like to introduce a new student to you. He's just transferred from Crystal City Junior High School and will be with us for the rest of the year. Everybody say hello to . . ."

No. Please. Not him. Not now. Did I say my life couldn't get any worse? I was right. It couldn't get worse, but it could get terribly, terribly worse by, like, a hundred times.

". . . Mandrake Steel."

There he stood in front of the class. Tall. Handsome. Muscles. Great hair. And all the power and confidence of a really great smile.

"Do you know who that is?" I asked Miles.

"Yeah, Gary. The teacher just said his name was Manbake Style or something. Who cares?"

I looked around the classroom. The girls were already writing love notes.

I leaned closer to Miles and whispered into his ear, "Also known as Charisma Kid."

"No way!" Miles erupted.

I smacked his shoulder and pulled him back down into his chair.

"Dude, I just violated every rule, bylaw, dictum, regulation, promise, and suggestion of being a sidekick. I don't need you blabbing it to the world. There's a reason they're called *secret* identities!"

"Apparently, not to you," Miles said sarcastically.

". . . and I just want you all to know how

excited I am to call Clearwater High my new home!" Charisma Kid finished.

Sure, no one else in the room knew he was Charisma Kid, but they didn't need to. I mean, they call him *Charisma* Kid for a reason.

I heard some girl titter. I turned around to see who the unfortunate soul was. Prudence Cane not only tittered but practically *swooned* when Charisma Kid flashed a toothy grin her way and winked.

Charisma Kid made his way down the aisle and as he passed me, he cracked a small smile. "Good to see you again, Spuddy."

"His name is Gary," Miles defended.

Charisma Kid sat behind Prudence.

"This is so cool," Miles said, leaning closer to me. "Maybe he'll let me sit at the same table at lunch. Or maybe even sit *next* to him! I've always wanted to meet a sidekick!"

"*I'm* a sidekick!" I whispered in a sharp tone.

"Yeah. To a pumpkin."

"Didn't you listen to *anything* I said? Haven't you been paying attention?" I hissed under my breath.

"What? What?" Miles defended. "I *told* him to call you Gary."

I dropped my head onto my desk with a defeated thud.

"Okay, class," Mr. Lang began, "let's review the Pythagorean theorem — yes, Mandrake?"

Charisma Kid raised his hand and waved it over his head. "I don't mean to interrupt, sir, but I just wanted to tell you what a striking tie you're wearing."

"Do you really think?" Mr. Lang asked, looking down at his tie. "I wasn't really sure . . . I mean when I picked it out at the store . . . Do you really think?"

"Absolutely. In fact, if you teach half as well as you pick ties, I'm in for quite an amazing learning experience."

Mr. Lang stopped for a moment, possibly feeling more handsome than he ever had in his life, and popped open his algebra book with renewed zeal.

"Was that the sweetest thing, or what?" Prudence Cane said to no one in particular.

With those eight words, no, wait. Seven. Uh . . . yeah . . . seven words, I realized I was in for the fight of my life. One where I was helpless to use my powers, and at stake was something more precious to me than the safety of the world.

Prudence Cane.

Chapter Three
Evil Is Bad

"Sssh!" Earlobe Lad hissed at me and covered his enormous ears.

"I didn't say anything," I whispered back.

"No. But the blinking. The blinking is driving . . . me . . . insane!"

I sat in my chair doing my best to not blink. It was always like this when I was on monitor duty with Earlobe Lad. His oversized ears and super-hearing made him hypersensitive to even the tiniest noises. The fact he had short hair only seemed to make his ears that much larger. His costume was green with a large ear on the chest.

My eyes started to water. Earlobe Lad glared at me. My lids quivered. Earlobe Lad clenched his teeth. I squinted, doing my best to relieve the burning pain that shot through my eyeballs. After, oh, one minute, I finally cracked like a cheap vase.

Blink-blink.

"Gah!" Earlobe Lad shouted at me, clutching his ears. "You did that on purpose!"

"I have to blink."

"Do you? Do you!?" he cried, standing from his sidekick chair, an accusing finger jabbing at my face.

"Calm down," Spice Girl said in a hushed voice. "He didn't do it on purpose."

"You're all against me," Earlobe Lad said as he slumped in his chair and slid beneath the table, "because I have giant ears!" The final words fell out of his mouth wrapped in despair — the despair that went hand-in-hand with giant ears.

I guess, anyway. My ears are normal.

The three of us sat at the Sidekick Super Table of Meetingness. Spice Girl had short blond hair. Her outfit was entirely pink with a purple "Girl Power" patch stuck on the front. I could smell the scent of Chamomile wafting up from her.

"It's good for headaches," she whispered to me.

It's usually about now — when Earlobe Lad is sobbing or Exact Change Kid is handing out two quarters, three dimes, two nickels, and ten pennies for a dollar, or I'm buffing the second coat of wax on the Pumpkinmobile — that I ask myself, "What was I thinking?"

I'll tell you what I was thinking. Imagine being a hero. Imagine saving people and being on the cover of magazines and stuff. Like, what if people looked up to you and wanted to be like you because you were so cool. That's what I was thinking. Smash evil and be popular. I had no idea I'd be doing laundry and listening to people whine all the time.

These are the battles TV never tells you about.

"What's with Elephant Boy?" Boom Boy asked as he entered the Clubhouse.

"I hate when you call me that," Earlobe Lad whimpered from under the table. "And stop breathing so loud."

Boom Boy had a cool power: he could blow up. The only problem was, if he blew up, he *really* blew up, so he could only do it once, if you know what I mean. His costume was pretty cool, too. Red and black Spandex. On his chest was a picture of himself blowing up.

"You guys ready for another boomtastic day of monitor duty? I get the front chair!" Boom Boy said, sniffing at Spice Girl.

"How do we know you even *have* the power to blow up?" Earlobe Lad whispered from under the table.

"What? What? Because if I couldn't blow up, I'd call myself 'I-Can't-Blow-Up Boy,'" Boom Boy sneered. "Or, if I had a really stupid power, I'd call myself Earlobe Lad."

"Makes sense to me," Spice Girl commented.

"Yeah, but I mean, we've never actually *seen* you blow up," Earlobe Lad whimpered. "No one has. You tell us you can blow up. Sometimes you even threaten that you'll blow up, but no one's ever actually *seen* you blow up."

"Stop messing with me or I swear I'll blow up," Boom Boy threatened.

"See."

"Okay! Okay! So that's how it's going to be, huh? Well, don't blame me when they're picking pieces of you off the ceiling," Boom Boy called back.

"Won't they be picking pieces of you off the ceiling, too?" Earlobe Lad pointed out.

"Yeah. But I'll have the satisfaction of being right."

Boom Boy stepped back from the table and balled his fists. His face grew redder and redder as he clenched his eyes.

"Maybe we should stop him," Spice Girl whispered nervously.

"No way," I responded. "I wanna see this."

"But what if someone . . . gets hurt?" Spice Girl warned.

"Of course someone's gonna get hurt! Boom Boy's about to blow himself up!"

Earlobe Lad crept out from under the table in time to see Boom Boy's face turn stop-sign red.

"Wow. He's really going to do it this time," Earlobe Lad whispered in a nearly inaudible voice.

"Wait!" Boom Boy said and opened his eyes. "I get it now. I get it. You *want* me to blow up don't you? Yeah. 'Cause once I do, I'll be gone and then there'll be no more Boom Boy to push around."

"But no one pushes you around," Earlobe Lad murmured.

"And that's how it better stay, because if they do, I swear I'll blow myself up!"

"I think *I'm* going to blow up," I said and smacked my palm against my forehead.

"You have that power, too?" Spice Girl asked.

Before I could answer, Boy-in-the-Plastic-Bubble Boy rolled into the Sidekick Super Clubhouse in his Giant Hamster Ball of Justice.

"Mmmph pah mm mm!" Boy-in-the-Plastic-Bubble Boy shouted from inside his protective ball, whose thick walls muffled his shouts like he had a sock in his mouth.

"What?" I yelled back.

"Ahh! You're killing me!" Earlobe Lad moaned.

Boy-in-the-Plastic-Bubble Boy pointed wildly toward the door. "Mmm! Mmmph! Mmm!"

"I dunno," Boom Boy said, scratching his chin. "I think he's trying to tell us something."

Boy-in-the-Plastic-Bubble Boy's face flushed red. In a fit of frustration, he began beating his head against the inside of his Giant Hamster Ball of Justice.

"Oh! Oh! I know this!" Spice Girl enthused. "It's Morse code! He's trying to tell us something about cheese."

Something was wrong and it was something more terrible than Boy-in-the-Plastic-Bubble Boy needing to use the bathroom. But before Boy-in-the-Plastic-Bubble Boy could shout one more word of nonsense, a huge explosion shook the Sidekick Clubhouse and would have rattled the Sidekick Clubhouse windows — if we had some.

"Don't look at me," Boom Boy said as the echo died. He checked himself over to make sure his arms and legs were still attached.

Exact Change Kid ran out from the Sidekick Super Bunk Room. "What the heck was that? It knocked over all my change piles. I've got pennies mixed with dimes mixed with nickels! It's madness!"

"Come on!" I shouted.

"Wait," Exact Change Kid called out, shuffling four dimes, two nickels, and a penny in his hand. He had a crew cut, was thin, wore bottle-thick glasses, and was decked out in white Spandex with red boots. "Don't you think we should have some rally cry before we run into battle?"

"How about, 'Let's go!'" I offered and turned to run.

"That's not very catchy," Spice Girl replied.

"Let's vote on Speedy's suggestion." Exact Change Kid raised his hand. "All those against, raise your hands."

Everybody but me raised their hands.

"Okay . . . that's four against."

"Look, I don't care what our rally cry is! I'm just saying let's go!"

"We just voted out 'Let's go,' Speedy. Please

don't try to push your ideas on the rest of us," Exact Change Kid whined.

"How about, 'Sidekick Summons!'" Spice Girl cheered.

"I don't know," Exact Change Kid said. "It has a ring, certainly, but there's just something . . . I don't know . . ."

"Mmmph Mmpah?" Boy-in-the-Plastic-Bubble Boy offered.

"Could be. Could be," Exact Change Kid replied, considering the suggestion.

"Look," I interrupted impatiently, "you guys vote and I'll check out the explosion. Someone may need help!"

I raced out of the room at 50 miles per hour and dodged left to avoid smacking into the wall.

"You should fill out the absentee ballot first!" Exact Change Kid called out after me, waving a blank form in the air.

I raced across the field and to the front of the League of Big Justice Headquarters of Big Justice. And then I saw it. I never thought this could happen. I never thought this would happen.

The League of Big Justice Headquarters of Big Justice was destroyed. This was what Boy-in-the-Plastic-Bubble Boy was trying to tell us.

I raced inside. Rubble was everywhere.

"Pumpkin Pete? King Justice? Lady Bug?" I called out. "Captain Haggis? Librarian? Ms. Mime? Is anybody here?"

Then I realized that if Ms. Mime were here, she wouldn't answer anyway.

"I am, worm," a voice growled behind me.

A man stepped out from the shadows of the rubble. I recognized him immediately from the League of Big Justice's Big Justice Super Crime Files.

The Professor.

Dressed in a black cap and gown, wire-rimmed glasses, and holding a pointer stick, The Professor looked nothing like that guy from "Gilligan's Island." And I'm sure he was nowhere as smart.

Plus, he was evil.

"Pop quiz," The Professor said. "What's faster? The fastest man alive or a laser?"

"Actually, I'm faster than the Fastest Man Alive Man. In fact, he changed his name to —"

"Idiot! I was using the phrase as a noun-modifier, not a proper noun," The Professor sighed.

I snickered. "Whoa! Hold on there, egghead. Save that grammar stuff for Spelling Beatrice."

"Oh, shut up!" The Professor snarled. His

pointer stick glowed red for a brief moment and in a flash, a laser shot from the tip.

I dove to the right and narrowly avoided becoming a melted slag heap. The Professor blasted again. I raced behind a wall of what used to be the League of Big Justice's Super Kitchen.

This was bad. There was no way this guy could've taken out the entire League of Big Justice alone. Were the other bad guys still here? There's no way I was ready for something this intense.

"Pop quiz," The Professor called out from the other side of the wall. "What's dressed in blue and yellow and will soon be quite a dead fellow?"

Dressed in blue and yellow? Duh.

"That's an easy one! Me!"

Me!?

I dove away as The Professor's graduation cap flew through the wall, blasting it to pieces.

Now I knew why they called it a *mortar*board.

Think, Guy! Think! This is bad. He's long-range. I've got no room to get speed. I can't dodge him forever. Gotta lure him outside. But how?

"What do you want from me?" I yelled out from my cover.

"I want you to die."

Well, at least he was honest.

"If you surrender now, I promise you a quick death," The Professor called out as his mortarboard cap flew back into his hand like a boomerang.

A distraction? Then run outside?

I took a rock and tossed it from my hiding place. The Professor spun and, without a moment's hesitation, blasted the rock into nothingness.

That's it! I got it. And this'll work, if he doesn't kill me first.

I ran out from my cover and raced across the large hall, weaving in and out of rubble while dodging The Professor's laser blasts. I finally dove for cover behind another shattered wall.

That's when The Professor went for his mortarboard again. He flung it like a Frisbee. I watched it zip through the air directly at my shelter.

I had to time this perfectly.

At the last second, I mustered all my speed and raced from cover. One great thing about being the fastest person in the world is that it means everyone else in the world is slower than you. I snatched the mortarboard from mid-air, spun like Michael Jordan, and flung it back toward The Professor.

The Professor's eyes widened like balloons.

He raised his pointer stick and, in more instinct than thought, blasted his own mortarboard.

The explosion threw him against a far wall, where he slumped to the ground.

"School's out," I said, standing over his unconscious body.

Okay, so maybe that wasn't so witty. But that's why my nickname isn't Pun Boy. And now that I think about it, I'm pretty darn happy about that.

I checked The Professor for something, anything, that could tell me what had happened here. Who or what could have taken out the League of Big Justice so quickly and easily? The thought sent a chill down my spine.

I checked his gown. That's where I found it. The card.

BROTHERHOOD OF ROTTENNESS

THE PROFESSOR

Member since 1999

Wow. I don't know where rottenness ranks between evil and bad, but I didn't like the sound of that. I guessed they took out the League of Big Justice and left The Professor behind to deal with the sidekicks.

Took out the League of Big Justice? What was I up against? I'm just a sidekick, a rookie, a —

"Sidekicks Strike!"

I spun around to see Exact Change Kid, Earlobe Lad, Spice Girl, Spelling Beatrice, and Boom Boy race into what was once the League of Big Justice Main Hall. I could hear Boy-in-the-Plastic-Bubble Boy's Giant Hamster Ball of Justice bang repeatedly against some rubble out in the hallway.

"Speedy! Speedy! Thank goodness!" Exact Change Kid called out as he ran up to me with dire urgency. "I just wanted you to know 'Sidekicks Strike' is not official yet, so don't feel left out . . . hey," he added, finally looking around. "Did we miss anything?"

"No," I said. "This is just the beginning."

Chapter Four
Punching Evil in the Face

"What do we know about the Brotherhood of Rottenness?" I asked the group.

"Well . . ." Spice Girl began. "We know they're a brotherhood!" She clapped her hands together like she'd just won a prize on a game show.

"And rotten, don't forget that," Boom Boy added sarcastically.

"Oh yeah, that, too." Spice Girl deflated, disappointed she hadn't thought of that first.

Exact Change Kid shuffled ten dimes and four pennies in one hand and typed at the Sidekick Super Computer with the other. "No records of them here."

"Let's interrogate The Professor," I suggested. "He'll tell us where the secret base of the Brotherhood of Rottenness is."

"Yeah, yeah. That's a boomtastic idea," Boom Boy said, hitting his clenched fist into his open palm.

After I had defeated The Professor, we tied him up and confiscated his pointer stick and gown so he couldn't use them to escape. We also answered one very important question: they *do* wear underwear under those outfits.

"You won't get anything from me, worms!" he boasted.

"Let me handle this," Boom Boy replied and took a dramatic step forward. He looked down on The Professor and cracked his knuckles. "You better tell us how to find the Brotherhood of Rottenness, or I swear, I swear, I'll . . . I'll . . ."

"You'll what?" The Professor asked defiantly.

"I'll blow myself up!"

"You wouldn't dare!" The Professor dared.

"Wouldn't I? Wouldn't I?" Boom Boy yelled back. "I'll blow up so good, there won't be enough left of you to teach kindergarten!"

"Go ahead!"

"Okay! Okay! But don't say I didn't warn you!" As Boom Boy clenched his fists and his cheeks began to flush red, Exact Change Kid casually turned and headed for the front door of the Side-kick Super Clubhouse like he was stepping out to get a sandwich from the fridge.

"Where're you going?" I asked.

"If Boom Boy's going to blow himself up, someone better be around to clean up the mess."

He had a point. Not about cleaning up the mess, but about still being around after Boom Boy blows himself up.

"Hold on," I said. "I'm coming with you."

"Wait!" Boom Boy said and opened his eyes. "I get it now. I get it. You *want* me to blow up, don't you? Yeah. 'Cause once I do, I'll be gone and then there'll be no more Boom Boy to save the League of Big Justice."

Boom Boy's awesome sense of redundancy never ceased to amaze me.

"Mmaa pahp maaap paaam ma?" Boy-in-the-Plastic-Bubble Boy said, rolling in front of Boom Boy to take over the interrogation.

"What?" The Professor asked.

"Mmaa pahp maaap paaam ma?"

"What?" The Professor repeated.

"Mmaa pahp maaap paaam ma!?" Boy-in-the-Plastic-Bubble Boy asked once more, this time louder and with a tinge of threat. Or at least as much threat as a boy in a giant hamster ball could muster.

"I'm sorry, but the bubble, it's just . . . could you possibly speak louder?"

"Nooooo!" Earlobe Lad screamed and raced from the room, crying.

"MMAA PAHP MAAAAP PAAAM MA!" Boy-in-the-Plastic-Bubble Boy yelled at the top of his lungs.

The Professor looked at the other sidekicks. "Is it me?" he asked. "Can someone clue me in here?"

"Maybe we should ask him what his favorite color is?" Spice Girl asked, anxious to help with the interrogation.

"Blue!" The Professor quickly replied, eager to speak to anyone but Boy-in-the-Plastic-Bubble Boy.

"See! That's not so hard!" Spice Girl clapped her hands together in a fit of victory. "Now let's ask him about Popsicles!"

Boy-in-the-Plastic-Bubble Boy fell against the inside of his Giant Hamster Ball of Justice and slid to the bottom like an unhappy little hamster who finally realized he wasn't getting anywhere on that hamster wheel of his. Exact Change Kid patted the outside of the Giant Hamster Ball of Justice.

"Mmm maa maph . . ." Boy-in-the-Plastic-Bubble Boy sadly groaned, taking a soapy shower in the cold, bitter waters of defeat.

"I know, B-I-T-P-B-B," Exact Change Kid consoled. "Evil teaches them well. He's a tough potato to crack."

Exact Change Kid paced back and forth in front of The Professor. He stopped, stared at The Professor for a silent moment, then rotated on his right heel and paced back the other way. The Professor tracked his every movement, waiting for the lion to pounce. Exact Change Kid paced to the right, pivoted, then paced back to the left, pivoted, paced back to the right, pivoted, then paced bac —

"Super Penny Surprise Attack!" Exact Change Kid screamed and pelted The Professor's face with pennies.

They bounced off his forehead and fell to the floor like bugs ricocheting off a windshield.

"Don't think . . . I won't use . . . nickels . . ." Exact Change Kid threatened between breathless huffs, exhausted from the effort.

The Professor didn't say a word.

"Any ideas?" I asked Spelling Beatrice.

"I *was* going to throw my Scrabble tiles at him, but if the pennies didn't work . . ." She opened her hand to reveal a fistful of vowels and consonants. There were twelve tiles total, but they could never spell "doubt" as well as the look on Spelling Beatrice's face.

"Hold on to your subordinate clause," I advised her. "I've got an idea. Give me a *Q*."

"*Q*!" Spice Girl shouted. She jumped up and down like a cheerleader, kicking her legs in the air. "What's that spell? *Q*!"

Spelling Beatrice slipped a *Q* Scrabble tile into her hand. She cupped it in her palm and we walked past Exact Change Kid, who was on his hands and knees retrieving the remains of his Super Penny Surprise Attack. "We'll get him next time, Abe," he mumbled under his breath.

I was going to let The Professor go, but secretly drop Spelling Beatrice's tile into his robe pocket. We'd be able to track the homing beacon that was in the *Q* tile with Spelling Beatrice's tracking *T* tile.

That was one cool thing about Spelling Beatrice. Some of her tiles actually did things — unlike Exact Change Kid's change, which was only good for lame things like pay phones and parking meters. Oh, and throwing them at evil's face.

Like, the *E* tiles were also tiny explosives, and if she attached the *R* tiles to her glasses, not only did it make her look like an idiot walking around with a square "R" over each eye, but it gave her infrared vision as well. I think the *Z* tile was best of all. It didn't have any special properties, but it's worth ten points in Scrabble. Slap that baby down on a triple-letter-score square and you're home free!

Anyway, that was my plan. Yeah, it was lame, but simple plans usually are. Problem was, before Beatrice could give me the *Q,* the wall exploded.

"Anyone seen Boom Boy lately?" I asked as the rubble and dust settled at my feet. Luckily none of it was pink and squishy.

Chapter Five
Evil Doesn't Knock Before Entering

"Oh, man! What's that smell?" Boom Boy asked.

"Eet iz zee ztink of eveel!" Le Poop shouted in a thick French accent as he and The Complainer entered the Sidekick Super Clubhouse through the gaping hole. "Filling up your nose like a very ztinky zing which fills up your nose like ztinky zings do!"

"You think it's bad now? Try spending the day with him," The Complainer complained, jabbing a thumb toward Le Poop. "And really, couldn't you have your clubhouse in a little more convenient location? The drive over here is a killer."

Clearly, they were here to save The Professor

and finish the job he had failed to do. Evil's funny that way. It rarely has time to do the job right the first time, but it always has time to do the same job twice.

I wasn't about to wait for them to make the first move. "Sidekicks Strike!" I shouted and raced toward The Complainer.

"That's not official yet!" Exact Change Kid offered the two minions of evil.

"Why are you attacking me first?" The Complainer griped. "He's the one who smells like rotten eggs!"

Le Poop exhaled. A green cloud gushed from his mouth and hit the ceiling. The toxic fumes loosened the roof and a large chunk collapsed to the floor. Spelling Beatrice and Spice Girl dove to the left and narrowly avoided being crushed.

I raced by The Complainer at 45 miles per hour and delivered three super-fast right hooks to his jaw.

"Hey! Do you have to hit so hard?" The Complainer protested.

He balled his fists and thrust them both outward. An energy blast shot out toward me. I had to skid to a stop, and my ankle twisted. Pain shot through my leg and I dove at the last second, letting the deadly blast shoot over my head.

Boy-in-the-Plastic-Bubble Boy wasn't so lucky.

"Pamh ma ma!" He yelled and charged forward like a see-through bowling ball. The blast hit his Giant Hamster Ball of Justice. It bounced backward, smashed into the back wall and rolled over Boom Boy, who, it seemed, was preparing to blow himself up again.

Boom Boy fell to the floor unconscious. The pinball ride knocked out Boy-in-the-Plastic-Bubble Boy, too. We were already down two and the fight had just begun. I was so desperate, I considered calling for Earlobe Lad.

"Smell this!" Spice Girl shouted and countered with a sharp odor of lavender and peaches at Le Poop.

"Mon Dieu!" he screamed. "Zuch a zpringtime fresh zent!"

Spelling Beatrice dug into her tile bag and pulled out a *D,* an *I,* and five *M*'s. And for evil, that spelled trouble. Well, actually it spelled *DIMMMMM* or *MMIMMDM,* but I'm saying, for *evil,* it spelled trouble.

"I'm going to split your infinitive!" she yelled, tossing the Tiles of Justice with the proficiency of a blackjack dealer.

The *D* and *I* tiles burst in a flash of blinding light. Le Poop covered his eyes and never saw the five *M* tiles shoot webbing among themselves to create a giant net that landed on him.

"Ha!" Spice Girl laughed. "You lose."

But a mere net would never stop the awesome stench of Le Poop. He raised his arm and unleashed the full power of his Armpit of Evil. The stench burst from his sweaty pit and melted the net.

"Oh, that is so gross!" Spice Girl said, plugging her nose.

"Where's Bar-of-Soap Boy when you really need him?" I joked.

"He quit last summer. Had to move someplace where it didn't rain so much," Spelling Beatrice explained, not realizing I wasn't serious.

The Complainer wasn't laughing either. He and Exact Change Kid were squaring off. They circled each other, waiting for the other to make his move.

"Washington Wrecker!" Exact Change Kid shouted, and he flung a fistful of quarters at The Complainer, who countered with a blast so fierce, it flung Exact Change Kid across the Sidekick Super Clubhouse and smashed him against the wall.

Dozens of pennies, dimes, and nickels clattered to the ground and rolled across the floor as

Exact Change Kid fell unconscious in a pile of loose change.

"Hello? Would it kill you to say 'Nice job, Ira,' just once?" The Complainer wailed to Le Poop. "Is it so hard to just say 'Thanks, Ira?' Why do I even bother?"

Things were getting bad. Spice Girl would have to handle Le Poop alone. Spelling Beatrice and I went after The Complainer. She launched an all-vowel attack while I used my super speed to kick debris from the destroyed wall like soccer balls.

Meanwhile, Spice Girl had shifted into peppermint and was driving back Le Poop's foul stink attack.

"You're smelly and I don't like you!" Spice Girl warned as she threw a layer of cinnamon into her assault.

Le Poop staggered. His knees began to shake. The sweet smell of good stung his evil senses.

"*Sacre bleu!* You are ztinging my evil zenses!" he cried.

See? I told you.

Le Poop spun around. I thought he was going to run. Boy, was I wrong. Spice Girl closed in for the final blow: sandalwood. But it was too late.

"Spice Girl! Nooo!" I yelled, but even my super speed couldn't save her.

Le Poop bent over. Spice Girl never had a chance.

The smell was so bad, even Boom Boy's eyes watered — and he was still unconscious. Le Poop broke wind and Spice Girl fell before its stinky awesomeness.

"Now you lose like zomeone who eez no good at winning," Le Poop gloated.

The moment Spice Girl fell to the floor, Spelling Beatrice plugged her nostrils with a Scrabble tile noseclip (an *A* tile and a *B* tile held together with a clothespin) and tossed me my own pair.

"Puht dem on doh dose!" she called out, her nostrils safely pinched closed.

"What?" I said.

"Doh dose! Kwip dem on doh dose!"

"'Dodos?' What's this got to do with the bird?" I asked.

"Not da buhd! Doh *dose!*" she stressed.

The Complainer stepped up next to me. "I think she wants you to put that thing on your toes," he explained.

"My toes? That doesn't make any sense," I replied.

"Hello? 'Thanks for trying to help.' 'I appreciate the suggestion, Ira,'" The Complainer grumbled. He shook his head. "Why do I even bother?"

Suddenly, the stink of Le Poop's fart floated into my area. My upper lip began to quiver, and I quickly figured out what Spelling Beatrice was yelling.

"Oh! Maah *dose!*" I said, clipping the tiles onto my nose and blocking Le Poop's attack.

"Dake Dah Combainer! De Boop id bine," I ordered Spelling Beatrice.

"Oh, what? Now I'm not good enough to fight?" The Complainer complained.

I raced around Le Poop, faster than he could rotate with his butt in the air. He wasn't able to track me. The speed caused a vortex of debris to spin wildly around Le Poop. He raised both his arms to launch a double-pit attack, but a large piece of debris swept up by the vortex hit him in the temple and ended his stinky reign of terror.

I turned to help Spelling Beatrice with The Complainer, but suddenly the roof caved in.

The last thing I saw before the rubble fell on me was the laughing face of The Professor, smoking pointer stick in hand and the rope that once held his wrists at his feet.

I dug myself from the rubble. I was bleeding, but not too badly. They had left me for dead, trapped under a ton of collapsed ceiling. The Professor and The Complainer had revived Le Poop and taken the other sidekicks.

One thing that's really cool about being fast is that sometimes you can do things faster than people can see. So after The Professor blasted the roof, I dove for cover under the Sidekick Super Computer desk.

And I made it.

It didn't protect me completely, but enough to save my life — and if you ask me, that's more than you can expect from furniture purchased at a yard sale.

"More money for me!" Pumpkin Pete had gloated when he stuffed the leftover twenty-dollar bills in his pocket. We had spent an entire Saturday driving from garage sale to garage sale looking for new Sidekick Clubhouse furniture.

Every bone in my body ached, but I had a job to finish. I had a whole lot of saving to do, and I was alone.

And then I heard the groan.

It was Exact Change Kid. He had been buried beneath the rubble as well. He was a little more beaten up than me, but otherwise okay. I helped him up.

"Thanks, Speedy," he moaned. He looked at the mess of rubble and scratched his head. "It's going to take forever to find all my pennies."

"Don burry, dahm dure dere are benty mo in da Thidegick Thuber Gouch dofa gushions."

Exact Change Kid gave me a blank stare. "Huh?"

Spelling Beatrice's Scrabble tile nose clip! I took it off and tried again.

"Don't worry, I'm sure there are plenty more in the Sidekick Super Couch sofa cushions. Come on. We've got to save them."

"How?" Exact Change Kid asked.

Sometimes, you don't worry about the how's. Sometimes you just have to dive in and hope things sort themselves out. When people are in danger and you are their only hope, it's really one of those times.

"Look!" I spotted a *T* tile on the ground by the huge hole in the far wall. Good old Spelling Beatrice had left her tracking tile behind, hoping someone would be able to use it. "We can track the homing *Q* tile that Spelling Beatrice still has!"

"Quick!" Exact Change Kid said, and I was very surprised, as I didn't think "quick" was even a word in his vocabulary. "To the Sidekick Super Rocket of Blastingness!"

"We have a rocket!?" I said, shocked.

But Exact Change Kid didn't answer. He raced toward the hole in the wall, and I ran as fast as I could with my throbbing ankle.

"Oh. Wait a sec," he said, stopping.

Exact Change Kid walked to a door on the far side of the Sidekick Super Clubhouse and knocked.

"What?" an irritated voice called from inside.

"Who's in there?" I asked Exact Change Kid, having always thought that that door was just a closet.

"Latchkey Kid," Exact Change Kid replied and cracked open the door.

"Hey, me and Speedy are going out for a bit, okay?"

"Okay . . . ," Latchkey Kid replied. He sat on a couch, watching TV, his eyes never leaving the screen.

"There's some leftover meat loaf in the Sidekick Super Freezer of Frozen Justice," Exact Change Kid told him. "Just put it in the microwave on high for four minutes, okay?"

"I know! I know!" Latchkey Kid spat back.

"You know, it's a beautiful day out. Maybe you could go to the park or something?"

"Yeah. Whatever."

"Okay. We'll see you around nine o'clock," Exact Change Kid told him. "If it's any later, we'll call, and then maybe you can have Mrs. Johnson come over."

Latchkey Kid didn't answer. He stared at the TV and took a swig from his soda. Exact Change Kid slowly closed the door.

"Maybe we should call a sitter?" he asked.

"Come on!" I urged and pulled Exact Change Kid through the gaping hole in the wall.

We raced across the Sidekick Super Additional-Parking Parking Lot of Justice.

"Where's the rocket?" I asked.

Exact Change Kid raced up to a cardboard box and crawled inside.

What awaited me inside was not an elevator that would take us down to the ultra-technology level of the Sidekick Super Clubhouse. It wasn't a transporter that would beam us to the bridge of the rocket. It wasn't even a go-cart with a chipmunk running on a treadmill as the engine.

"This isn't a rocket!" I yelled. "This is just a cardboard box with knobs and dials painted on the inside!"

Exact Change Kid hung his head, broken by the pounding hammer of reality. "I know, I know," he sobbed. "I was hoping no one would notice."

I crawled out of the box and kicked it. My foot broke through the cardboard side.

"Oh, great!" Exact Change Kid shouted from inside. "Now it'll never get off the ground!"

Spelling Beatrice's tracking tile beeped in my hand. It grew faint. "Come on! The signal's fading! They'll be out of range soon!"

The two of us raced from the parking lot and stood on the street corner. I could run there myself, but my ankle was still hurting from being buried under the rubble, and I had to save all my strength for the final battle.

And there *would* be a final battle. I wasn't about to give up.

"There!" Exact Change Kid shouted, pointing down the street.

"What?" I said. "It's just a bus."

"Just a bus to you. A fortress of solitude to me!"

The bus pulled over at the curb and we raced inside.

"Sir, by the power vested in me through the use of Spandex, I'm commandeering this bus for the battle against evil!" Exact Change Kid told the driver.

"Whatever," the driver said, pulling from the curb. "That'll be two dollars and ten cents. Each. *Exact change only.*"

Exact Change Kid leaped in front of me and thrust out his arms as if he was protecting me from a charging bull.

"Stand back, Speedy," he said, filled with determination and purpose. "Stand back and watch me shine!"

Back at the Sidekick Super Clubhouse, Earlobe Lad raced into the main room.

"EVERYBODY! LOOK!" He shouted and pointed to a pair of giant lead earmuffs wrapped around his head. "NOW YOU CAN TALK AS LOUD AS — HEY . . . WHERE IS EVERYBODY?"

The microwave beeped. Latchkey Kid looked up from behind the open door of the fridge.

"They'll be back around nine," he said, popping open another can of soda.

"Amazing."

"What?" Exact Change Kid asked, raising his sullen head from his hands.

"It's just amazing, that's all. Absolutely amazing."

"What is?" he asked again.

"Nothing. It's nothing," I replied.

Exact Change Kid hung his head again. This time it sunk a little lower between his knees than before.

"Let me ask you a question," I began, trying my best to not yell. "If I could *not* run fast, and I mean really, *really* fast, do you think I'd call myself Speedy!?"

"No." Exact Change Kid whimpered.

"Then why in the world does a sidekick named Exact Change Kid NOT have one hundred percent exact change the only time in his stupid life he'll ever really need it!?"

Okay. I was shouting now.

"I didn't know my utility belt was back in the rubble. How do you expect me to have exact change without it?"

"Then maybe you should call yourself Exact Change Utility Belt Kid!"

"That's a stupid name . . . although Exact Change Utility Belt *Boy* does have a nice ring to it."

The two of us sat on the curb. We'd gotten half a block before the driver had kicked us out. "Exact change only!" He laughed as the door hit me in the butt on the way out. "And happy Halloween."

"Now what?" Exact Change Kid asked. "I hate to admit it, but I'm not much good without my change."

"*Without* your change? I don't know where you've been for the last two hours, but you're not much good *with* your change, either!"

Okay, that was a little low and the moment I said it, I felt bad. But I was on edge, and when I'm on edge I do edgy things.

I felt my ankle. It still hurt too much to use my super speed. Sure, you might be able to walk on a sprained ankle, but try running 90 miles per hour on one. I had to use my brains. It was the League of Big Justice's only hope.

Use my brains!? The League of Big Justice didn't stand a chance.

"Do you still have your cell phone?" I asked.

Exact Change Kid pulled a phone from one of his hidden pockets. Time seemed to stop as I faced one of the most difficult choices I had ever made. Once I dialed, there'd be no turning back. Spelling Beatrice's beeping *T* sounded in my hand, as if to remind me my sacrifice meant nothing if it saved lives. I pressed the phone to my ear.

"Hi, Mom? I need a favor . . ."

Within fifteen minutes, my mom arrived in her Oldsmobile station wagon. We climbed into the car.

"Guy tells me you throw pennies," my mom said as Exact Change Kid buckled his seat belt.

Trust me. It just went downhill from there.

Spelling Beatrice's tracking tile did the job and led us directly to the secret base of the Brotherhood of Rottenness. It was hidden in a garbage dump. How fitting.

At least for Le Poop.

I was hiding behind a small mound of flies, leftover pizza, and something that might have been alive at one point but now was just kinda stinky. Exact Change Kid was across the street getting change at a mini-mart.

And my mom was in the parking lot.

I had told her this was just a training drill. If I had told her the truth, there was no way she would have let me go anywhere near the garbage dump. She parked in the lot to wait for our "drill" to be over so she could take me home.

At least I'd convinced her to stay in the car.

From my hiding place, I had watched the evil ones carry Boom Boy, Spice Girl, Spelling Beatrice, and Boy-in-the-Plastic-Bubble Boy through a large hidden door, and I was waiting for Exact Change Kid to return before we attacked.

That's what I *wanted* to do, but the thing about evil is, it just seems to have a mind of its own. The large door started to slide closed. Once it did, I knew there would be no way for us to get into the base. It was now or never.

I bolted from my hiding spot. Pain shot through my ankle, but I ignored it. I had to. With each super-speed step, the pain stabbed higher up my leg. The door didn't care how much my ankle hurt. It was closing. I pushed my speed up to 72 miles per hour and dove, barely sliding past the threshold as the door slammed shut and cut me off from the rest of the world.

That's when things really got bad.

Everything started to shake. That's never good when you're in a building, because buildings that shake when there's no earthquake can only mean one thing: Two Ton Tom was attacking.

I turned to face his artery-clogged attack, but he wasn't there. I was alone. So if a building shakes and Two Ton Tom isn't attacking, then what that really means is that the building isn't a building.

It's a rocket ship.

Below, Exact Change Kid raced up with a fistful of dimes. "Take that!" he shouted, and he flung the coins at the ship as it ripped away from its garbage-covered camouflage and slowly lifted into the sky.

I peered through a window in the ship's side. The last thing I saw was Exact Change Kid covering his head as the dimes fell back to earth and rained down on him like candy from a broken piñata.

He waved at me. "I'll just go wait in the car!"

Chapter Eight
Showdown with Evil

Once I was inside the ship, it didn't take long to find the League of Big Justice and the sidekicks. A few left turns and one hydrolift later, and I was on the ship's bridge.

And so were they: King Justice, Lady Bug, Captain Haggis, The Stain, Mr. Ironic, The Good Egg, Ms. Mime, Depression Dave, The Librarian, Pumpkin Pete, Charisma Kid, Spelling Beatrice, Spice Girl, and Boom Boy were all in large glass tubes. Boy-in-the-Plastic-Bubble Boy hung from the ceiling like a giant hamster disco ball.

Everyone seemed to be okay, but they looked like they were in a trance. Probably something in the tubes. I ran over to the console and looked for a button to free them.

And there was a button. There were also about a hundred knobs and two hundred levers. This thing was more complex than my last science test.

I quickly scanned the console. I didn't have much time. One way or another, the Brotherhood would find me. I spotted a red button and hovered my finger over it.

The thing about red buttons is, pushing them always makes something really good or something really bad happen. Red buttons never result in something just okay. You never push a red button and then say "Gee. That was okay." Try it and see.

"I wouldn't pick that one if I were you," a voice behind me said. "Unless you want to start the dishwasher."

I knew that the moment I turned, I would be face to face with the evil mastermind that had defeated the League of Big Justice! Such a feat would take the greatest supervillain the world had ever known! He would be big, strong, mean, and terrifying with a genius mind capable of defeating the League of Big Justice and putting the heroes in tubes like Barbie and Ken dolls in a

Toys 'R Us! I braced myself and turned, realizing I could never be fully prepared to face the awesome evil thing that waited to unleash the full fury of its awesome evilness and stuff.

"Hey!" I said. "You're just a puppet!"

"A puppet, or the greatest evil force the world has ever known!?"

I looked at him. He was made of wood and had strings. "No. Just a puppet. So, can you let my friends out or what?" I asked, looking at the balding chubby man with bottle-thick glasses who controlled the puppet's strings.

"Why are you talking to him!?" the puppet shouted.

"Because . . . he's a human being and . . . you're made of wood?" Seemed like a no-brainer to me.

"He's my mind slave!" the puppet shouted again. He looked up to the chubby man and cackled with glee. "Aren't you . . . mind slave?"

"Yes . . . master . . ." the chubby man said.

Oh, brother.

"Yeah. Sure. Mind slave. Silly me for missing that one."

"Allow me to introduce the architect of your demise!" the manic puppet said. "I am . . . Peenoh Keeoh!"

"Don't you mean 'Pinocchio'?" I asked.

"Yeah. If I want to get slapped silly with a lawsuit. Idiot!"

One thing you can always count on a villain to do is explain his plan. There's this thing about bad guys, like they never got enough attention as kids or something, so any time someone will listen to them, they just blab, blab, blab. That's why they always have lackeys and minions. Those poor stooges have to sit around and listen to their bosses yak all the time.

It's like people going to a Michael Jackson concert. You don't know why they do it, but it just keeps happening.

"You're probably wondering why I did all this?" Peenoh Keeoh asked.

See. Even puppets need attention.

"I plan to shoot the League of Big Justice and their lousy little sidekicks into the heart of the sun! I will be the man who killed the League of Big Justice! Then I will take my diabolical puppet satellite and blast the earth, turning everyone into living puppets!" Peenoh Keeoh cackled again like a mad jackal and then coughed.

"So, let me get this straight. You defeat the League of Big Justice, defeat the sidekicks, then take everybody here, put them in tubes, blast them into space and now . . . *now* you're going to shoot them into the sun? And after all that, you're just going to zap the earth and turn everyone into puppets? And . . . this makes sense to you?"

"What's your point?"

"I mean, why didn't you just leave all of us back on Earth and just turn us into puppets when you zapped everyone else?"

"Hello? Did I say my name was Mr. Plan? No. I don't think so. When you battle Dr. Oh-What-A-Great-Plan-I-Always-Make and his League of Immaculate Strategy, feel free to criticize. But for now, save the commentary. . . ."

Wow. I never realized it before, but sometimes evil is stupid.

". . . So, after I shoot all of you into the sun, I will place Phase II of my master plan into motion."

I grabbed a metal box that was magnetically anchored to the floor and raced to King Justice's tube. I wasn't sure how strong the glass was, but I was hoping that with enough speed, I could shatter it. I ignored the fact my ankle was about to burst and swung the metal box at the tube while running 48 miles per hour.

"Wait! What are you doing?" Peenoh Keeoh

yelled. "I'm not done revealing my master plan. Stop and listen to me talk!"

Here's a little clue for you. Never listen to the speech. When you're flying toward the sun and your teammates are trapped in tubes, don't wait until the end of the speech. It's just a time killer until the villain can finally laugh and say, "Ha! Ha! And now you're too late to save them!" Then he pushes a button, most likely red, and everyone blows up. But if you smash the tubes *while* he's talking and he's nowhere near the blow-up button, then he just gets real angry because he can't gloat anymore.

Trust me on this one.

The metal box hit against the tube and . . . nothing. I hit it again and only managed to crack the exterior.

"Idiot! That's not ordinary glass!" Peenoh Keeoh laughed. "It's . . . well . . . I don't know what it is exactly, but it's really strong and I got it on sale at Construction Depot."

I whacked the tube a few more times. Peenoh Keeoh shook his head and looked up to his mind slave.

"They never listen, do they?" Peenoh Keeoh sighed. "Okay. Moving on . . ."

I ignored Peenoh Keeoh and pressed my hands

against King Justice's tube. I used my speed to vibrate both my hands super fast. The tube rattled violently and shook so hard the cracks grew and grew. My muscles stung and I felt my arms cramp. I couldn't keep it up much longer.

Peenoh Keeoh's wooden mouth dropped open. He hit the alarm button as the tube finally shattered. King Justice collapsed to the floor and I nearly joined him. My arms ached as if both my shoulders were dislocated.

"Nice . . . work . . . Sporty," King Justice said.

He took a few deep breaths and regained his senses. King Justice rose. He towered over me. His chest emblazoned with the colors of the American flag, he stood as a constant reminder of justice and virtue.

"Prepare to taste the Five Knuckles of Goodness, Peenoh Keeoh!" King Justice yelled.

In quick succession, King Justice used his super strength to shatter the tubes imprisoning the other members of the League of Big Justice and the sidekicks.

"Not so fast, you monolithic moron!" Peenoh Keeoh shouted, pointing behind King Justice. Eight towers of evil stood in the doorway like eight really evil towers standing in a doorway.

Le Poop. The Complainer. Jellyfish. The Professor. Mayham and Rye. The Dentist. Santa Claws. These were the deadly members of the Brotherhood of Rottenness.

"Ho-ho-horror!" Santa Claws growled and extended the steel claws in his hands. A bell tinkled at the end of his red cap and his belly jiggled like a bowl full of jelly.

Peenoh Keeoh jumped up on the console and pointed at the heroes.

No. Don't say it. Anything but those two words that every villain always says at these moments. The two words that should be banned from a villain's repertoire along with the gloating laugh and the slow-moving death ray.

"Get them!"

There. He had to say it, didn't he?

"Time to deal justice from the card deck of impartiality!" King Justice called out and leapt into the fray.

The battle royale was met!

The Dentist whipped out his drill. "No novocaine for you!" he yelled and attacked Captain Haggis, who countered with a mighty blast on his Bagpipes of Righteousness.

Santa Claws slashed at The Stain while Charisma Kid flashed his pearly whites. Le Poop rematched with Spice Girl and Spelling Beatrice.

The Complainer attacked Ms. Mime, who confused him by pretending to walk against a strong gust of wind. Mayham and Rye took on The Good Egg and King Justice while The Professor blasted Mr. Ironic with his pointer stick. Mr. Ironic used his reflective powers to bounce the blast back at The Professor.

"Look! I've used your own power against you!" Mr. Ironic boasted.

Depression Dave slumped in the corner and sat next to Jellyfish, who just quivered. "What's the use in fighting," Depression Dave said to the spineless mass on the floor. "I'd just lose anyway."

Pumpkin Pete raced to the console, hoping to turn the ship around.

That left me . . . and Peenoh Keeoh. He leaped from the console and landed on my back. The little marionette of madness wrapped his puppet strings around my neck and pulled.

"Whose plan stinks now?" he laughed.

I grabbed Peenoh Keeoh by his tiny wooden hand. "Your reign of terror is over, tiny wooden doll!" I shouted and tried to throw him across the room, but the strings on his controller tightened, and Peenoh Keeoh's mind slave adjusted the puppet so he landed nimbly on his feet.

"Somehow, I think the chubby guy's got

something to do with the little wood dude!" Pumpkin Pete called out, looking up briefly from the console and referring to Peenoh Keeoh's mind slave.

Mayham and Rye had cracked The Good Egg and came to help their evil wooden leader. Even with a good ankle, I couldn't go one-on-three. Or even one-on-two-and-a-puppet.

"Pumpkin Pete! I need your help!"

Pumpkin Pete's large orange head peeked up from behind the console. "I'm right behind you . . . uh . . . Running-Really-Fast-Kid!" He slowly lowered his head back behind the console.

"Just give up. We should all just give up," Depression Dave mumbled in the corner. "Isn't that right, Squishy Fish Thing?"

I wasn't sure if Jellyfish understood, or what the heck Jellyfish was supposed to be, besides a jellyfish, but he, or she, or it, just quivered and let out a thick bubble of mucus.

Mayham used his massive fists to try to smash me into the floor, but I zipped to the side, where Rye waited with her toasting fire power. It singed my skin.

Rye released a larger fire blast. I didn't have

time to think. I just reacted. I ran toward Mayham so fast, it created a wind channel that sucked Rye's blast after me. Mayham raised his ham-sized fists to pound me, but I dodged to the side at the last instant. The fire trailing behind me seared Mayham's face. He swung blindly and clobbered Rye, knocking her unconscious. Mayham stumbled across the room where King Justice took care of him.

"Pumpkin Powers, activate!" Pumpkin Pete shouted and leaped out from behind the console. "Whew. That was a close one," he said and went back to pushing buttons on the console.

Things looked bad for the Brotherhood of Rottenness. The Good Egg, The Librarian, Lady Bug, Boom Boy, Spelling Beatrice, and The Stain were down for the count, and The Stain was ruining the carpet as well. But the Brotherhood was down to Santa Claws, Le Poop, The Dentist, and Peenoh Keeoh.

Oh, yeah. And Jellyfish.

"The lawnmower of justice has cut down the weeds of your evil, Peenoh Keeoh!" King Justice yelled. "Give up, or prepare to feel the stinging grains from the sandpaper of good, you malicious Muppet!"

"I've got more than one splinter for you," Peenoh Keeoh growled.

"Bring it on, pinecone boy!" King Justice replied.

The two sides squared off. The final dance was about to begin, and baby, I was *so* ready to tango!

Chapter Nine
The Ninth Chapter

EXIT

"Hey! I think this button will send us home," Pumpkin Pete said, oblivious to the final battle which was about to take place. Pete's long, vine-like fingers stabbed down on the lone red button that sat in the middle of the console. "That settles that!"

The ship shuddered. A bright red ray blasted from the front and shot down to Earth. Pumpkin Pete had just turned the state of Ohio into puppets.

"I didn't do it!" he gasped.

"Uh . . . Pumpkin Pete? Maybe you should lay off the buttons for a while?" I said.

"Nonsense! My keen pumpkin senses have

revealed the *one* button not to touch," Pumpkin Pete reasoned and pushed another button.

"Airlock seals to self-destruct in T minus three minutes and counting . . ." a computer voice chimed.

"And now my keen pumpkin senses have revealed a *second* button to not touch," Pumpkin Pete added, scratching his giant gourd head.

"So . . . what happens now?" I asked.

"Well . . . in two minutes the airlock seals blow and we all get sucked into space and popped like human balloons," Peenoh Keeoh answered, shrugging his puppet shoulders. "Except for me. I'm made of wood."

"Don't worry. We can just swim home," Spice Girl assured King Justice.

Everybody stood for a moment and stared at each other, not sure how to absorb this unforeseen turn of events. Santa Claws nonchalantly whistled "Jingle Bells" and slowly shuffled toward the door.

"T minus two minutes and fifty seconds . . ."

Suddenly Santa Claws bolted for the door and raced out of the main room. Le Poop, The Dentist, and Peenoh Keeoh — with his mind slave, of course — quickly followed after. Peenoh Keeoh stopped in the doorway.

"You've destroyed Ohio and yourselves!" he shouted, then raced down the hall.

"Wow. That is so ironic," Spice Girl said.

"Actually, it's more of a coincidence," Mr. Ironic corrected.

"You're right, it *is* a coincidence," Spice added. "And that's what makes it so ironic."

"League of Big Justice! Sidekicks! Evacuate!" King Justice yelled and hoisted The Good Egg and The Stain over each shoulder like they were sacks of flour.

"You don't have to tell me twice!" Pumpkin Pete said and raced from the room, arms empty. "Pumpkin feets, don't fail me now!"

The rest of us grabbed or roused an unconscious hero or bad guy and ran to the escape pods. Depression Dave found a shovel and scooped up Jellyfish, who seemed to quiver with gratitude.

"T minus two minutes . . ."

Warning sirens blared through the ship as we ran to the escape pods like kids playing musical chairs. Each pod could only hold three people, so it would be tight. I saw an open pod door and raced over.

"Sorry! Only room for one!" Pumpkin Pete said, "And I have a big fat head. Like a pumpkin!" He hit the door seal and left me in the hall.

"Over here, son!" King Justice called out.

I raced to his pod and climbed in. It would be close, but it looked like all of us were going to be safe.

"T minus one minute and forty seconds . . ."

"That was close, King Justice, sir."

"It sure was, Sporty. It sure was."

So get this. I was riding in an escape pod with the founder of the League of Big Justice. So he didn't know my name exactly, but "Sporty" was close enough. I wondered if now would be a bad time to ask for his autograph? Boy, would that just kill the other sidekicks when I showed them? I could just hear them all *oooh*-ing and *aaah*-ing. Heck, that would probably be the first and only time I ever understood what Boy-in-the-Plastic-Bubble Boy was trying to tell me. I could just see Boy-in-the-Plastic-Bubble Boy's face . . . when . . . he . . . Boy-in-the-Plastic-Bubble Boy . . . when he . . . Boy-in-the-Plastic-Bubble Boy . . . Boy-in-the-Plastic — oh my gosh!

"We forgot Boy-in-the-Plastic-Bubble Boy!" I yelled at King Justice as he was about to hit the door seal. "We left him stuck to the roof in his Giant Hamster Ball of Justice!"

"T minus one minute and thirty seconds . . ."

"Stay here, son," King Justice said. "Don't wait for us. Sometimes soldiers don't return from the war."

"You'll never make it!" I warned him. Then I said something really surprising. No, not "Leave him," which may have been a better idea. I didn't even say, "My mistake, he was never here!" No. What I did say was, "Only my super speed has a chance! *I'll* save him!"

I think the ship's thin air was getting to me.

"You're not going alone," King Justice replied.

I touched his shoulder and looked into his eyes.

"Earth needs a King," I said. "And Justice needs you."

Oh, brother. Who knew I'd be so corny T minus one minute and ten seconds before I got sucked into space and popped like a human balloon?

Chapter Ten
Sucked into Space and Popped Like a Human Balloon

"T minus fifty-five seconds . . ."

"Shut up!" I yelled at the computer voice.

"Mmmmaph maaa!" Boy-in-the-Plastic-Bubble Boy shouted down to me from his Giant Hamster Ball of Justice that still hung high above the deck by a steel chain.

So this was the end. Everybody was safely on their way to Earth in the escape pods while I paced beneath the human Christmas tree ornament that dangled from the ceiling. I knew the job was dangerous when I took it, but, and this may sound crazy, I never thought I would really get hurt. Heroes aren't supposed to get hurt. That's why they're heroes.

But in the real world, they do. And maybe that's what really makes them heroes — because they're not perfect or superhuman; because they bleed and break like everyone else; because they might die, but they still rush into danger.

King Justice was right. Sometimes soldiers don't return from the war.

"T minus fifty seconds . . ."

No. I may not return from this war, but I sure was going down fighting! I wasn't going to quit. I would never quit, no matter the odds! I used my super speed to leap onto Boy-in-the-Plastic-Bubble Boy's Giant Hamster Ball of Justice. No throbbing ankle pain could stop me now.

"T minus forty-five seconds . . ."

I landed near the top of the Giant Hamster Ball of Justice and immediately slipped down the side and fell to the floor.

"T minus forty seconds . . ."

It was a tough decision, saving Boy-in-the-Plastic-Bubble Boy or smashing that stupid computer voice with a crow bar. I couldn't do both. Luckily for Boy-in-the-Plastic-Bubble Boy, I didn't have a crow bar.

I tried again, racing even faster. I slapped against the ball and started to slide down the side again. I strained my arm muscles and stretched my hand in a frantic effort to grab the chain that held the ball in place. My fingers reached like a lazy man desperately stretching for the TV remote that fell off the couch.

"T minus thirty-five seconds . . ."

Inches. Tiny inches to go. Boy-in-the-Plastic-Bubble Boy pressed his face against the concave wall of his Giant Hamster Ball of Justice. His cheek squished like a bowl of pink Jell-O.

Maybe the cheek helped. Maybe my fingers were just a tiny bit longer than I had remembered, but I reached the chain and pulled myself up. At the very top was a release lever.

I pulled it. The Giant Hamster Ball of Justice fell and bounced hard on the deck below. I slid off the top, plopped on the ground, and was instantly crushed by Boy-in-the-Plastic-Bubble Boy as he rolled screaming for the door.

Some days it just doesn't pay to save anyone.

"T minus thirty seconds . . ."

"MMAA PAM MAM PAM MAM!" Boy-in-the-Plastic-Bubble Boy screamed as he banged his Giant Hamster Ball of Justice against the tiny doorway. I don't know how the Brotherhood of Rottenness got him into this room, but there was no way he was getting out; not without a jackhammer and twenty pounds of butter.

"You won't fit!" I shouted.

"Mmaa pam mam pam mam . . . ?" Boy-in-the-Plastic-Bubble Boy whined.

"Yeah. I guess so."

"T minus twenty-five seconds . . ."

So there I was, about to get sucked into space and . . . well . . . you know . . . and my last twenty seconds of life were being spent with a kid in a giant hamster ball who kept saying "Mmaa pam mam pam mam" over and over, as if I actually understood the difference between "mam" and "pam." I mean, he could've just said "pam pam pam pam pam pam pam." Made no difference to me. Why waste time and throw "mam" in there?

Why? Because that was just the kind of side-kick Boy-in-the-Plastic-Bubble Boy was. That's why.

"T minus twenty seconds . . ."

Maybe they'd build a statue to honor us. Or even have a "Death of Speedy" polyvinyl-chloride special collector's edition statuette for sale in the League of Big Justice Super Souvenir Gift Shop. They'd better at least retire my number.

"Here's your number," Pumpkin Pete had said to me at my orientation and handed me a Post-It with two digits scribbled on it.

"Twenty-six? What's this for?"

"If you die, we retire it. Like baseball."

"But no one dies in baseball."

"I know," Pumpkin Pete sighed. "That's why it's so boring."

So that's what I had to look forward to. Maybe a plastic toy and my yellow Post-It hanging on the wall in the new Planet Superhero restaurant, right next to Lipstick Lydia's mascara brush.

Why didn't I listen to my brother? Why didn't I become Junior Assistant Florist?

"Just think, you can run around and hand out flowers," he had told me.

"T minus fifteen seconds . . ."

Suddenly the large display screen clicked on and an enormous image of Peenoh Keeoh, filled the room.

"As you get sucked into space, King Justice, remember it was I, Peenoh Keeoh, who sent you there! That's right! The little puppet with strings destroyed the greatest good the world has ever known! I, Peenoh Keeoh, destroyed King Justice! Chew on that, King! Hahahahahahaha . . ."

"He's gone," I said to the screen.

"Hahahahaha — what?" Peenoh Keeoh cut his laugh short with a choking cough. "What do you mean he's gone?"

"He left in an escape pod."

"What!? When did this happen? Why wasn't I informed!?" Peenoh Keeoh turned his head and glared at his mind slave and then turned back to face me. "Then tell the rest of the pathetic League of Big Justice to step forward so they can look upon the face of their doom!"

"They all went with King Justice."

"So who am I killing then? The Good Egg, perhaps? Please tell me at least Ms. Mime is still there?"

"Nope. Both gone. It's just me and Boy-in-the-Plastic-Bubble Boy."

"So, let me get this straight," Peenoh Keeoh sighed and rubbed his pine forehead with his little wooden hand. "All I did was turn Ohio into puppets and kill a kid in a hamster ball and you!?"

"Well . . . technically . . . Pumpkin Pete turned Ohio into puppets," I corrected.

"Why do I even bother!?" Peenoh Keeoh moaned.

"Welcome to my life," Depression Dave grumbled, leaning forward so I could finally see he was in the same escape pod as Peenoh Keeoh.

Then the screen went black.

"T minus ten . . . nine . . . eight . . ."

The saddest thing of all was that I had only

nine more seconds to contemplate the love of my life: Prudence Cane. You couldn't think about her enough in nine lifetimes, and there I was with less time than it took to drive Earlobe Lad crazy to consider all things Prudence.

Man, is life unfair.

"Seven . . . six . . . five . . . four . . ."

I looked to Boy-in-the-Plastic-Bubble Boy. We both gave a brave nod to each other and prepared for the end.

"Three . . . two . . . one . . . airlock seals self-destruct."

There was a terrible groan from the ship, like its insides were being sucked out through a straw. The airlock seals on the outer hull blew, and the ship immediately began to decompress.

A tremendous suction filled the room and pulled me and Boy-in-the-Plastic-Bubble Boy toward the door. I raced against the suction as fast as I could but only managed to move several feet away. Boy-in-the-Plastic-Bubble Boy ran in his Giant Hamster Ball of Justice, but the power of the suction was so great, he just ran in place like he was on a hamster wheel.

"Faster!" I shouted to him. "Run faster!"

He redoubled his efforts, but to no avail. The

spinning Hamster Ball of Justice slowly slid toward the door — the last threshold between us and the vacuum of outer space.

Boy-in-the-Plastic-Bubble Boy fell to his knees, exhausted. Unable to fight against the suction, the tremendous force sucked the Giant Hamster Ball of Justice toward the opening.

This was the end.

The Giant Hamster Ball of Justice slammed hard against the door opening, and suddenly, the suction died. Without the incredible force pulling me back toward the door, I shot forward and smashed against the far wall.

I hit the console hard and slumped to the ground. The pain was intense, but it couldn't stop me from laughing. There, across the room, Boy-in-the-Plastic-Bubble Boy's Giant Hamster Ball of Justice — his wonderful, amazing, incredible, Giant Hamster Ball of Justice — was lodged in the door like a giant cork, cutting the room off from the rest of the ship.

While the remainder of the ship decompressed and was sucked into the vacuum of space, we were safe, a new seal created by Boy-in-the-Plastic-Bubble Boy.

He was laughing even harder than me. He was on his knees at the bottom of his ball. Tears ran down his red cheeks and he pumped a tri-umphant fist into the air.

And for the first time since I joined the Side-kicks three weeks ago, I finally understood what Boy-in-the-Plastic-Bubble Boy was trying to say.

"So then what happened?" Miles could barely sit on the lunch bench, he was so excited.

"Well, we lost a lot of oxygen before the room was sealed off, but I managed to find the auto-pilot and it took us back to Earth."

"Man! All I did last night was watch MTV. Did you get a medal or anything?"

"No. Everyone thought we were dead, so they gave the medal to Pumpkin Pete as my sponsor."

"But once they found out you were alive, didn't Pete give the medal to you?"

"What do you think? But it doesn't matter. The ribbon was so big because it had to fit around Pumpkin Pete's pumpkin head, it would've hung down to my knees."

"Yeah, I suppose." Miles took a bite of his sandwich. "So Peenoh Keeoh and the Brotherhood of Rottenness got away?"

"Some of them. We captured The Complainer, Jellyfish, The Professor, Mayham and Rye. . . ."

"Dude, you are *so* a hero! How does it feel?"

Until that moment, I really didn't think about it. I had saved the League of Big Justice and the Sidekicks and stopped Peenoh Keeoh's plan to turn everyone into puppets, but for some reason, I still felt the same. I was still Guy Martin.

"It feels, I dunno. Good?"

"That's it?" Miles blurted out, nearly dropping his milk carton. "Good!?"

"Okay! Real good."

"Hey, Guy." It was Charisma Kid in his Mandrake Steel secret identity. "Good to see you and the human cork got out okay."

"I bet you were losing a lot of sleep," I snorted.

"Real shame you didn't get any credit," Charisma Kid sneered.

"It's not about the credit . . . but neither did you!"

"Oh, I wouldn't say that," he laughed and

dropped the front page of the newspaper in front of me.

KING JUSTICE AND CHARISMA KID SAVE EARTH! the headline screamed. PUMPKIN PETE AWARDED MEDAL OF BRAVERY! a smaller one blared.

All the work I did, all the danger and risk and effort, and this is how everything winds up? Charisma Kid's overly attractive mug and perfect hair plastered over the front page of every newspaper in the nation, except for the one from Ohio that said AHHH! WE'RE ALL PUPPETS!

Now I know how Peenoh Keeoh felt.

"Good for you," I said and spilled the brown sauce from my Salisbury steak onto the picture.

Charisma Kid leaned over to pick up the paper. "Oh, and I won't be able to make the Sidekicks meeting today," he whispered in my ear to make sure no one could hear. "I have a date . . ."

"Good for you," I repeated, and tried to flick my cranberry cobbler into Charisma Kid's hair.

". . . with Prudence Cane."

Ouch.

"Good for me, huh?" Charisma Kid stood up and smiled.

I had to admit, the guy has great teeth.

Suddenly the Salisbury steak looked more

like the lump of mystery meat it really was rather than the tasty morsel it wanted so badly to be.

"Looks like you won't be able to follow Prudence Cane home today," Miles said.

"I don't follow her home!" I defended. "I just happen to go home the same way."

"But you live in the opposite direction, Guy."

"Shut up."

Where was Peenoh Keeoh's puppet ray when I really needed it?

So, maybe there has been a time or two when I've gone out of my way and strolled in the general direction of Prudence's house. I mean, I don't follow her in a creepy way. I just kinda . . . linger slowly behind her while she walks. That's not so bad, is it? And believe me, I'm not the only one. Some real losers follow her all over school.

Okay, so sometimes I follow her all over school, too. But she's totally hot! I mean . . . it's just . . . she's . . .

I am such a loser.

Chapter Twelve
The End

Guy's mom tapped the steering wheel with her index finger. She stopped after a few seconds and looked at the radio. She had given up on it hours ago, unable to find anything worth listening to. She adjusted the rearview mirror for the tenth time, then checked the gas gauge again. Finally, she leaned over the steering wheel and looked up through the windshield into the general direction where she had watched the ship take her son into the sky.

"Do you think they'll be back soon?" she asked.

"I hope so," Exact Change Kid replied. "I have to go to the bathroom."